MY SISTER ANNIE

My Sister Annie

by Bill Dodds

Boyds Mills Press

For Carrie
—B.D.

Published by Caroline House
Boyds Mills Press, Inc.
A Highlights Company
815 Church Street
Honesdale, Pennsylvania 18431
Printed in the United States of America

Publisher Cataloging-in-Publication Data
Dodds, Bill.
     My sister Annie / by Bill Dodds.—1st ed.
[96] p. : cm.
Summary : Growing up, trying to be accepted, and having a sister with
Down syndrome make life a challenge for Charlie.
ISBN 1-56397-114-3
1. Handicapped children—Juvenile fiction. 2. Down
syndrome—Juvenile fiction. [1. Handicapped children—Fiction.
2. Down syndrome—Fiction.]
I. Title.
813.54—dc20   [F]   1993
Library of Congress Catalog Card Number 91-77599

First edition, 1993
Book designed by Charlotte Staub
The text of this book is set in 12-point Garamond Light.
Distributed by St. Martin's Press

10 9 8 7 6 5 4 3

CHAPTER
1

THE FAMILY
I'M STUCK WITH

"C HUCKIE, CHUCKIE, CHUCKIE!" Two wide hands beat against the chain-link fence. "COME ON, CHUCKIE!"

I hate that name. My name is Charlie.

I looked over behind third base. I didn't have to. I knew she was there. Everybody at the playfield knew she was there.

"CHUCKIE, CHUCKIE, CHUCKIE!"

The parents in the bleachers seemed to think she was cute, probably because Annie still looks like a little kid.

She's thirteen, but she acts like she's four. I've

already got two sisters—twins—who are four. I sure don't need another one.

The guys on the field were probably glad she was on the other side of the fence.

"CHUCKIE, CHUCKIE, CHUCKIE!"

Why didn't Mom or Dad tell her to sit down and shut up! How was I supposed to pitch with her standing over there yelling at me? I looked over again, and there was our coach visiting with her. Like everything was just great, everything was normal. I guess in a way it was.

Not normal is normal with my family.

I called for a time-out, and the catcher ran out to the mound to talk to me. I knew he would. Anytime there was a break in the game, Bob Carbonetti would run out and talk to me. That's why he was catcher. He just *loved* doing that. And he never had anything to say.

"Take it easy, Charlie," he told me this time.

"Yeah."

"This guy is no hitter."

The count was one strike and three balls. There were runners on first and third. Top of the last inning. We were ahead by one run. We were the home team. If I could just hold them for another two strikes, we'd win the game and play for the league championship next Saturday.

I'm eleven and I'm a good pitcher, but I need to concentrate to get the job done.

"CHUCKIE, CHUCKIE, CHUCKIE!"

Annie slammed the fence.

"We're all rootin' for you, Charlie," Coach McCarthy shouted.

"No hitter, Charlie. No hitter," Bob said.

The kid at the plate had hit three times this morning, every time he came up to bat.

"He's got two singles and a double so far, Bob," I said.

"Yeah? Huh. Well, he can't get another one. Nobody's perfect."

"Come on, Chuckie," the kid at the plate yelled out to me. "Throw the ball."

"Go catch this," I said to Bob and gave him a little shove back toward home. I pushed him harder than I meant to, and he sort of tripped, and the Hornets—that's who we were playing—started laughing. I helped him up, and the umpire said, "Play ball."

Concentrate, I told myself.

"CHUCKIE, CHUCKIE, CHUCKIE!"

SHUT UP, ANNIE!

She banged on the fence again.

The kid at the plate—now batting a thousand, a perfect score, no matter what Bob said—was smiling at me. Laughing at me.

I threw the ball as hard as I could right at his teeth.

But I didn't have much control, and it went screaming over the plate.

The umpire called strike two, but Bob dropped the ball because it had come in so fast, and the runner on first ran down to second.

The kid at the plate wasn't smiling anymore.

"CHUCKIE, CHUCKIE, CHUCKIE!"

Bang, bang, bang.

I knew what Annie wanted. I had known all along. I just didn't want to give it to her. Sometimes it seems like she gets everything she wants. Mostly it seems like she wants to ruin my life.

I turned toward her and gave her a little wave. She gave me a big one back and then went to sit with Mom and Dad and the twins.

Great, Chuckie, I said to myself. You still have to get this guy out.

I didn't. He hit a beautiful one. Lucky for me it went right into our center fielder's glove.

We were in the league championship game.

I just wanted to go home and die.

Annie is my older sister, but she isn't. Older, I

mean. She was born before I was, but she's . . . she's different. And she's made me want to die lots of times since I first noticed how different she is. And sometimes she's made me so mad I've wanted to kill her.

I thought she was just like me and everybody else until one day—when she was seven years old—when I grabbed her by the back of her sweatshirt and pulled her down on her big fat butt. Annie weighed more than I did, but I was taller, even though I was only five. A little taller, anyway. Well, she landed on the curb and started screaming. Then she got up and waddled into the house and told Mom, and I didn't get to watch any TV for the rest of the day.

It wasn't fair. Annie and I had been playing catch, and she was about to run right out into the street.

A car was coming.

Fast.

I felt like a hero until she screamed and Mom screamed and nobody wanted to listen to a story about a fast car and a slow girl. About a ball rolling out into the street, and about Annie ready to charge right out after it. The ball got smashed into a pancake, but nobody wanted to hear about that.

I spent the evening in my room. I wrote out my

ABCs five times and looked at comic books.

That is the first time I remember knowing Annie was different, and I think I knew it the instant she hit the ground and yelled. She would have run right into the street. Right in front of the car. She should have thanked me. She sure didn't.

When we were driving home from the baseball game, Dad said we should all go out and celebrate my victory.

"No thank you," I answered.

"Our Charlie is saying no to ice cream!" he said to Mom as if he just couldn't believe it. "Check and see if he's got a fever."

Then they both laughed like that was just about the funniest thing in the whole wide world, and the girls laughed, too, even though I was sure they didn't know what they were laughing about.

"I want ice cream," Annie said.

"Me, too!" the twins screamed. I had one on either side of me in the backseat. They just about blew out my eardrums.

"Come on, Charlie," Twin Number One said.

"Yeah, come on," Twin Number Two said.

After the game they had each said they wanted to sit next to their big brother. Mom thought that was cute. It meant they got to sit by the doors. I got stuck in the middle, sitting over the hump.

I didn't think it was very cute.

Annie was up front. She always gets to ride up front. Otherwise she gets carsick. If she rides in the back, even over to the store, she throws up. (It takes a long time for a car not to smell like somebody threw up in it after somebody throws up in it. A long, long time.)

I think Annie can make herself throw up any old time she wants. I think she just wants to ride in the front seat.

"I want ice cream," she said again.

"Ice cream for everyone," Dad agreed.

See?

"I scream!" Mom said. "You scream! We all scream for . . ."

"Ice Cream!" they all yelled.

Not normal.

"Come on, Charlie," my dad said. "Loosen up."

He always says I take life too seriously—I need to loosen up. I figure Annie is loose enough. I have to be tight for two.

I was hoping we were just going to use the drive-through window at the Dairy Queen, but Annie and the little girls wanted to go inside.

The twins' names are kind of like a game my

mom likes to play. She calls them by any two things that go together. Salt and Pepper. Bacon and Eggs. Death and Destruction. She thinks that's funny. Sometimes it is.

They're identical twins. It's easy for Mom and Dad and me to tell them apart. Annie has some trouble with that and sometimes just calls whichever one she's talking to "Twin."

Other people say they look exactly alike. They don't. You notice a lot of things when you're a part of a family that you don't notice when you're not a part of it. A lot. Their real names are Rock and Roll. Just kidding. Open and Shut. Merry Christmas and Happy New Year. Fish and Chips. Their real names are Rhonda and Rhoda. No kidding. You can see why Mom calls them Oil and Vinegar.

One time after we had all been to the dentist, I called them Rinse and Spit. I thought that was a pretty good one. Mom yelled at me. I bet she would have laughed if she'd thought of it first.

I don't know how Mom and Dad came up with "Rhonda" and "Rhoda," but they did, so that was the end of that.

Anyway, as soon as we got inside the Dairy Queen, Annie and Ketchup and Mustard had to go to the bathroom. That was OK with me—I figured

I was just lucky Annie hadn't wet her pants.

Mom took them, and by the time they were back Dad and I had five big ice-cream cones waiting at a table. (I still wasn't in the mood to celebrate.) I was the one who had done all the work out on the field, but everybody got a cone. It didn't seem fair to me.

I was thinking about that and ignoring the girls when Mom said, "Isn't that a little friend of yours?" She was pointing out the window at some girl, and at first I thought it was somebody from school, but it wasn't. Just thinking about that "somebody" and a dance that was coming up made me start to blush, and then everybody in the family had to say, "How come you're blushing, Charlie?" nice and loud. Everybody in the place was staring at me.

I just sat there, and by then the girls' cones were dripping all over their hands and they were messing around. One thing led to another, and one of the twins—AM or FM—jabbed Annie in the face, and suddenly Annie had chocolate ice cream way up her nose.

She screamed, and while Mom was scolding the twins, Dad grabbed a napkin and held it over her nose and told her to blow. She sniffed instead.

Then she screamed louder.

Maybe she was freezing her brain. I don't know. I know she doesn't have a very big one. No, that's not right. It might be the same size as everybody else's, but it doesn't work the same.

Annie has Down syndrome. She's mentally retarded.

CHAPTER
2

A REALLY LOUSY
SUNDAY

I woke up early the next morning because
someone had crawled under my bed and was
doing a bad job of trying not to laugh.

Guess who.

"Go away, Annie," I said.

"I'm not Annie."

"Go away."

"I'm Rhonda."

"Go away."

"I'm Rhoda."

"Go away."

"I'm hungry."

I have a room to myself, but until I was almost seven, Annie and I had bunk beds. I was on the top. Annie was at first, but she fell out one night and sprained her wrist, and the doctor said she was lucky she didn't break her neck.

We had a lot of fun back then. She would wake me up early in the morning and we'd sneak down to the living room and watch cartoons or go to the kitchen and make our own breakfast.

We thought we were hot stuff.

I must have been about four—about the twins' age—when she and I decided our corn flakes had lost their crunch, and so we loaded up the toaster with a handful or two. I set it on "light." I thought I was so smart. The smoke started coming out almost right away. I knew we were in trouble. Annie didn't.

After the smoke came the smoke detector alarm, and after the smoke detector alarm—very soon after—came Mom and Dad.

"I'm hungry," Annie said again from under my bed.

"I don't care."

"Are you awake?"

"No."

"Wanna watch cartoons?"

"Go bug Peanut Butter and Jelly."

"Come on, Chuckie."

I opened my eyes and checked my clock. Five in the morning! Sunday morning!

"Annie, do you know what time it is?"

She crawled out and looked at my clock. "Five. One. One," she said.

"Yeah. In the morning."

"I'm hungry. You make me breakfast."

"Corn flakes," I said. "Extra crispy."

"Pizza!"

"Shh! You're going to wake everybody. You want me to call and get a pizza delivered on Sunday morning? At five, one, one?"

"Five. One. Two."

"Mom said nobody could get up before seven-thirty," I told her. "This is a long time before seven-thirty."

"Pizza."

Then I realized what she was talking about. In the refrigerator. Leftovers! Cold pizza: breakfast of champions. I guessed I was a little hungry, too.

"Look," I said, "I'll go down and get us some, but you have to stay right here. Don't do anything or say anything, because if you wake up Mom or Dad you're going to be in *big* trouble."

"All Right!"

"Shhh!"

She gave me a big smile. People always say she has a great smile. I guess she does. Kind of like a jack-o'-lantern. People with Down syndrome have really round faces, but I'm not saying that to cut her down.

I didn't know much about this stuff until I did a school report on it earlier in the year. Down syndrome was named for an English doctor more than one hundred years ago. He didn't have it. He just described what people who have it are like. They're mentally retarded. Maybe a little, maybe a lot. And they have slanted eyes and a flat nose and a small head and short, stubby hands. (Hands that can really beat on a chain-link fence.) Some of them have trouble with their heart or their breathing or their eyes.

Annie wears pretty thick glasses.

One person in 650 is born with Down syndrome. They have an extra chromosome.

After I finished writing my report, my teacher read it and said, "Charlie, what's a chromosome?" and I knew I wasn't finished.

A chromosome, I found out, is a part of a cell that has genes in it.

Genes say what color eyes you have and what kind of hair and all sorts of stuff. People with Down syndrome have forty-seven chromosomes. Other people have forty-six. One extra chromosome can really mess up a body.

Annie gave me her big smile, and I snuck down to the kitchen and brought back four slices of pizza. Then I made another trip and brought back the little black-and-white TV.

By the time I got back there was only one piece of pizza left. Part of one piece. She was chewing on it.

"Annie, you pig," I said.

"I was hungry."

"No wonder you're fat."

"Cartoons."

"Fatty."

She lifted my pillow. There were the other three pieces. She thought that was just about the funniest thing she had ever seen.

I would have laughed more if there hadn't been tomato sauce all over my sheet and pillowcase. I knew I'd have to be sure to stuff them way down to the bottom of the laundry hamper.

"Chuckie, you pig!" she said.

"Shut up."

"You're fat!"

"Shut up." I wasn't mad.

"Fatty!"

There weren't any cartoons on because it was

Sunday. Only guys preaching and guys sitting around talking and a nature film on the barn owl.

Annie started getting tired as soon as the food was gone. That was very soon. I pulled out my sleeping bag from the back of my closet and unrolled it, and she slept on the floor next to my bed until Mom woke us at seven-thirty and said it was time to get ready for church.

I guess she didn't see the TV set. She didn't say anything about it.

Every Sunday it's the same routine:

1. I get ready and wait.

2. Mom pushes Annie and the twins to hurry up and finish their breakfast and get their nice clothes on and not fool around up in their room and *hurry up!*

3. Dad sleeps in and then moves fast so that he's ready to go at the same time as everybody else. Sometimes he is, and sometimes he isn't.

4. We all get in the car and Mom asks Annie if she remembered to go to the bathroom and Annie says no.

5. After she's back in the car, we drive to church and go inside and sit on the left side up toward the front.

6. Mom sits next to Annie and tells her she has to be a good girl today.

7. Dad sits between the twins and tells them they have to sit still.

8. I sit next to the wall and pray nobody I know sees me with Annie and the twins.

9. Annie isn't good.

10. The twins don't sit still.

Every Sunday. For as far back as I can remember.

One thing made this Sunday stand out. After Mass, when the priest was out in the back saying good morning to people, he asked me, "How was the baseball game yesterday, Charlie? Did you win?"

And Annie said, "We kicked their butts!"

Sometimes on Sunday we go out to lunch. "Brunch," Mom calls it. That means she and Dad have breakfast. The rest of us have hamburgers.

Chip and Dale usually have a great time when we go out like that. So does Annie. The three of them use their spoons to get the ice out of their water glasses and blow the wrappers off their straws (usually trying to hit me without Dad's seeing them and usually being unable to do either). And they sneak little packs of sugar in their pockets to take home. And they put pepper in their hands and blow it at each other, trying to make the other person sneeze.

Sometimes I like going out. But sometimes I don't. This Sunday I didn't.

The problem started when the waitress came to take our orders and Mom said none of the kids could have soda pop. Just milk. Or nothing.

I thought, Fine. Nothing.

It didn't seem fair to me.

The twins howled a little bit, and Mom said it was because we had been having too many treats lately. We need good food.

I was going to point out that what we drink isn't a food, but that would have gotten Dad mad, so I didn't say anything.

"I wanna root beer!" Annie screamed.

Annie can be very loud sometimes. Very.

"Lower your voice, Annie," Dad said. "Now."

"Milk," Mom said.

"Why?"

"You need it to grow big and strong," Mom said.

"I Wanna Root Beer!"

By now the waitress had turned all red and she said, "We have diet root beer. There's no sugar in that." She was probably trying to be helpful. It didn't help at all.

"Milk," Dad said.

The twins and I just stared at the table. We had seen this lots of times before.

I knew the other people sitting near us in the restaurant would be staring at my family or seeming not to notice. How could they not notice!

Maybe if they were deaf and blind. And if they didn't feel the floor shake a little bit each time Annie kicked the leg of the table—which she had started to do.

Mom took hold of Annie's face in both her hands and put her own face right in front of it. "Milk or nothing," she said.

"Root Beer!"

"Nothing!"

"Root—"

I looked down. I knew what was coming next. Why didn't Annie?

Mom took Annie's hand, and the two of them walked out to wait in the car.

I wished we would all just leave. Just go home. Stay home.

I wasn't hungry. Not even for fries.

"I'll have the bacon and eggs," Dad said to the waitress, as if nothing had happened. "Scrambled."

She seemed a little scrambled herself, so he

repeated his whole order.

"And burgers and fries and milk," he added. "For three." For the twins and me. Annie would have just a plain old lunch at home.

"Yes, sir."

"And could you bring out a second order of bacon and eggs about ten minutes after I get mine? Eggs over easy."

"Yes, sir."

That was for Mom. Dad ate his breakfast very fast and then went out and took over guard duty in the car. Mom came back in and ate hers.

People looked at her as she walked by them, and I know they were thinking how glad they were they didn't have a daughter like Annie.

Or a sister.

But Mom didn't see them.

One of the first memories I have is riding in the shopping cart while she bought groceries. I'd be underneath, and Annie would be in the little seat, where Mom could grab her if there was a problem.

There was always a problem. Annie would yell or reach for stuff and knock something over or do something else to make Mom mad, and then we'd have to hurry up with the shopping and get through the checkout line and get in the car.

When we got older, I used to walk beside Mom, and Annie got to ride underneath the cart. Other people in the store would look down at her and then look again and kind of frown and then look at Mom and me.

Mom would smile and nod or just make her face turn to stone and not even see them.

I don't know how she does that. I wish I did.

But that wasn't the worst of it. While we were leaving the restaurant, I saw Brian, one of the guys from the Bombers. He was in there with his family.

We looked at each other, but neither one of us said a word.

I knew he had seen the whole thing. I figured my chances of finally getting to join the club were pretty much shot.

The Bombers were already in middle school. Seventh-graders. They all wore these bomber jackets. That's where they got their name. They were the top guns in the neighborhood.

Sometimes they treated me like a peewee because I was still in grade school, but other times they let me hang out with them. I had thought they were going to make me an official member, since I was almost done with the sixth grade, but now I really doubted it.

Allen was the leader. He was almost a whole year older than most of them because he started school late. He had moved into the neighborhood when I was five.

When he found out he and Annie were about the same age, he said, "Retardos must grow funny. She's little. And ugly."

All the other kids laughed.

I didn't know what to do.

"Your sister is an ugly retardo!" he said right to me.

I spit on him.

He hit me really hard—harder than I had ever been hit before in my life—and I went home and cried.

I didn't let Mom hear me, because I didn't want to get in trouble for fighting.

After that, Allen and the other kids would say mean stuff once in a while, but usually they didn't say anything about Annie. They didn't let her play with them, of course. She couldn't follow the rules, and she wasn't very coordinated.

They let me play sometimes, but only because I was pretty good at sports. Better than most of them, really. One of them would usually want me on his team.

It ended up that I kind of had two lives, one

playing with Annie, because we still had fun together when nobody else was around, and one with the guys. The only problem was when the two overlapped—like yesterday at the baseball game.

Some of the Bombers had had a game earlier, and they had stuck around to watch me pitch. They had lost.

I knew they were cheering for me until Annie started pounding on the fence and yelling "CHUCKIE!" Then they split. I saw them leave.

Now in the restaurant, here was one of them, Brian.

Shoot.

We were almost to the car when I remembered I had forgotten my jacket back at the table. I ran back in to get it. This time when I looked at Brian he made a goofy face and mouthed some words. His parents didn't notice. I knew what he had said.

"Root beer."

CHAPTER
3

How to Make
Girls Like You

The only good thing about going to school the next morning was knowing there were only two more Mondays left in the school year. I had been looking forward to summer, but now, after the root beer incident, I wasn't so sure.

It would probably blow over. Most of the junk Annie did that made my life miserable blew over eventually. Usually it was replaced by something new to be embarrassed about.

I do all right in school. I like it. Most of the time. Language Arts is my favorite. I know that makes some people think "Oh, gross!" but it's what I like.

Some people like science or math or something else. One kid in my class loves lunch. And he's very good at it.

What I really love about school is a girl I met last summer. Well, I didn't really meet her then. And I'm not saying I love her. I love thinking about her. She was the one who was on my mind at the Dairy Queen on Saturday.

I'm afraid I may be the only one who ever felt this way. I don't know why I do. I guess I'm going crazy.

Anyway, last summer Dad and I went to a high school baseball game, and there was this girl sitting in front of us, and I thought she looked really nice.

She was dressed really fancy for watching a baseball game. She had dark hair and a blouse with buttons up the back instead of the front. Unless she had her shirt on backwards! Ha!

Annie still does that. Puts her shirt on backwards or inside out or upside down. (Not upside down. I'm kidding about that but not about the other ways.)

This girl was really cute. I noticed one of her buttons wasn't buttoned, and so I leaned over to Dad and whispered, "Should I tell her one of her buttons isn't buttoned?"

And he said to me, and he didn't whisper, "I don't know, Charlie. That might embarrass her. Maybe she'd think you're getting a little too personal. How would you feel if she turned around and said to you, 'Your fly is open'?"

Jeez.

It wasn't. I checked.

I didn't say anything to her.

She and some big guy, her brother, I guess, left before the game was over. I thought that would be the last time I'd ever see her.

I was wrong!!!!

Girls are . . . hard to explain. Your mom and your sisters aren't girls. They are, but they're not. There's a difference. I can't explain it. A big difference.

So, anyway, I saw her last summer and thought I'd never see her again. Then she showed up at my school last fall. She was out on the playground talking to Allen, the Bomber Kid from my neighborhood. He goes to the middle school that's right across the street from my grade school. She was looking closely at his Bomber jacket. She seemed to be very impressed.

It turned out she and I were in the same grade, but different classrooms. There are three sixth-grade classrooms at my school.

I don't think she recognized me. She was wearing a different blouse. I saw her in the hall and didn't say anything to her. For three weeks I just looked at her.

I didn't used to like girls. No, that's not right. First I didn't even notice if people were boys or girls. Then I noticed, but I didn't care. Then I cared. I didn't like girls and I only liked boys. Then, lately, all I've noticed is girls, and I think about them a lot!

I had thought about the Blouse Girl all summer. That's why I couldn't talk to her. I just couldn't.

Finally, one morning before the bell rang, she was standing all alone, and I walked over to her and said, "Hi." Pretty good!

And she said, "Hi."

I felt great all day.

Since then we've said hi almost every day, and I've found out her name is Misty. Isn't that a beautiful name?

These are other conversations we've had:

I said, "Is that your pencil?"

And she said, "What?"

And I said, "On the ground."

And she said, "No."

That was around Thanksgiving. At Christmas, I said, "I wish I brought my gloves."

And she said, "It's really cold today."

I remember all this stuff because I've kept a journal for the past year and a half. It's helped me remember every word, but I don't think I would have forgotten any of it anyway.

What all this is leading up to is that the class was having a dance Saturday night and I wanted to ask Misty if she was going, and if she was going, would she dance with me.

And I wanted to ask her, if I got really brave, if she would dance only a fast dance with me or would she dance a slow dance with me, too.

I had only one week left to find out.

So on the big morning I dressed very carefully. And when my mom said, "You're going to wear *that* to school?" I must have looked pretty good.

I like school because at school I'm the oldest. Not the oldest there. Not even the oldest in the sixth grade. I'm almost twelve, but there are other kids who have birthdays before I do.

I'm the oldest because there are times every year when the teacher says, "I want those in the class who are the only ones from your family here to take this note home to your parents. If you have an older brother or sister, don't take one. They will be bringing it home." And I take a note home.

At home I'm not the oldest, but I am. Annie is

older than I am, but she acts a lot younger. And talks and looks and works and thinks a lot younger. In some ways she's closer to Pepperoni and Black Olives than to me.

Last week they were trying to teach her the alphabet with the "A, B, C, D, E, F, G" song.

Annie did all right until she got to "L, M, N, O, P." It came out more like "L, ma nem, ma nem, O, P."

The twins just laughed and laughed and so did Annie. They were having a lot of fun. They sang that song at least one hundred times. At least.

Annie learned to write her name at the special school she goes to. She does go to school, just not the one I go to. So I'm the oldest one in my family at my school, and I like that.

Nobody compares me with Annie at school.

When Mom and Dad do that I get mad. But they don't know it. Because when they compare me with Annie they say either "You're a lot smarter than Annie. You have to do very well" or "Quit showing off and making Annie feel bad."

Not those exact words, but that's what they mean.

Sometimes when I show them a good grade on a test or writing project, they just look sad. They say "That's wonderful!" but they don't look like they think it's so wonderful.

The smarter I am, I guess, the dumber I make Annie look. I don't mean that to sound mean, but I think it's true.

That's why I like going to school and being on my own. Nobody compares me with anybody else at school—except with other normal kids. I like that.

Some of the kids in my class don't even know about Annie. Sometimes I like that, too. I'm sorry, but I do.

Monday morning I was all set, sort of, to ask Misty if maybe it was a possibility that she might think about considering dancing a slow dance with me.

I saw her out on the playground before school and was going to walk up and ask. I think I was. That was my plan. I might have done it. Really. Things didn't work out.

I took about two steps and heard "Root Beer!" from across the street at the middle school.

It wasn't Annie. It was the Bombers, Allen and Brian and the guys. Brian must have told them about it. I bet they all had a good laugh. They were laughing now.

The Bombers crossed the street and stood on the other side of the playground fence.

Misty was talking to some other girls now.

"Charlie," Allen said, "Brian says he saw you at breakfast."

"Brunch," I said.

"Huh?"

"Nothing."

"Enjoy your milk?"

He and the other guys laughed. There were about five or six of them. It sounded more like twenty or thirty.

"Sisters," I said, hoping that would cover it.

A couple of the guys nodded.

"Who needs 'em?" I added.

"No lie," one kid said.

"I'm coming to your school Thursday night," I said to Allen.

"So?"

"Open house."

"Right," he said. "For the new kiddies."

"We'll be there," another kid, Joey, said. "Mr. Henson asked some of us to hang out in wood shop and show you wimps some of the stuff men can do."

"Uh-huh," I said. "Saturday night we're going to have a dance. Here at school."

They didn't look too impressed. Why was I trying to impress them? Why the heck did I care what they thought about the world? Or about me? How do I know? I cared.

"We got time for a smoke?" Allen asked one of the guys.

"Bell's gonna ring," he said.

Allen nodded like life was so unfair. Like didn't it just figure there wasn't enough time for a cigarette before the morning bell rang?

He stuffed his hands into his jacket pockets and turned and walked away.

Man, I wanted a jacket like that! It was imitation leather with an imitation sheepskin collar. If I got into their club, I could wear one just like it.

Girls really liked guys in those jackets. That's what the guys said, anyway. It couldn't hurt. And I was willing to do just about anything that would help.

Especially with Misty. Who, by now, had disappeared.

Allen and the guys were back across the street. He turned around and yelled at me: "You up for an initiation this week?"

He meant into the club.

"YEAH!" I hollered back.

He nodded again. Not a "life isn't fair" nod but an "all right, guy" nod. Then he turned away.

The bell rang.

It hadn't been a bad morning after all. I didn't talk to Misty, but I was a lot closer to being a Bomber. And how could she refuse a guy in an imitation leather jacket with an imitation sheepskin collar? Not a bad morning at all.

I stayed after school and helped Miss Blum correct some papers. She's the second-grade teacher. I had been helping her correct spelling papers and arithmetic and stuff since after Christmas. It was something to do. It was kind of fun.

By the time I got home, Annie's bus was just pulling up in front of the house. She takes it to and from the special school she goes to. It's for kids who have all kinds of stuff wrong with them. Their bodies or their brains don't work right. Or both.

"CHUCKIE!" she said when she hopped off and saw me.

"See ya, Annie!" the bus driver said before he slammed the door shut.

"'Bye, Milton!"

"Annie, my name is Charlie," I said. I wasn't mad. She just forgets a lot.

"I know."

"So how come you always call me Chuckie?"

"Charlie is my Chuckie," she said, and I had no idea what she meant so I let it go. I went inside to talk to Mom. She was busy preparing dinner.

"The Bombers say I might get to join them this week," I told her.

"Aren't those boys a little rough?" she said.

"They're OK," I said, and she didn't say anything. "If I get in, I can wear a jacket like theirs."

Now it's true I could have worn one anyway. It's a free country. But that would have been like buying a Super Bowl ring or an Oscar.

"Those flight jackets?" Mom asked.

"Yeah."

"They give you one?"

"No, I buy it."

"You have enough money for one of those?"

I doubted it. "I don't know," I said. "I thought maybe you and Dad would help me pay for it."

"How much do you have saved?"

Saved? About . . . nothing. "Not a lot," I said. That was the truth.

"Those leather jackets cost a lot of money, Charlie," Mom said.

"Not leather. Imitation."

"Those aren't cheap either, honey."

I didn't say anything.

"Maybe Dad and I can help you get one that's nylon."

"NYLON!" I shouted.

"That's about the most we can afford right now, honey."

Stinko.

CHAPTER
4

SORT OF SHOPLIFTING

When I woke up Tuesday morning I knew I felt bad about something, but I couldn't remember what.

Then I remembered. The jacket. And I started feeling even worse.

I decided to think about Misty instead. This would be the day I would talk to her about the dance. What if she wasn't even going? Then I'd *really* feel bad. I decided not to think about that possibility.

I think Mom and Dad were surprised I didn't whine about the flight jacket during breakfast.

Annie jabbered away, and the twins both spilled their milk.

I didn't much notice. I was too busy saying to myself, Hi, Misty. Are you going to Saturday's dance? I'd like to dance with you.

Maybe, if I was really brave, I'd change it to, Hi, Misty. Are you going to Saturday's dance? I'd like to slow-dance with you.

"Do you feel all right?" Mom asked, and she put her cool hand on my cheek.

"Yeah," I said.

"You look a little flushed. Maybe you have a fever."

"I'm OK."

I think I was blushing from just thinking about asking Misty to dance. I decided maybe I'd better plan on using the first version. It wouldn't be that tough. Hi, Misty. . . .

There she was, on the playground. All alone, before school. It was perfect.

All I had to do was go over and give my speech.

This was it. It couldn't be better. She was still all alone. Nobody else was around her. And Allen and the Bombers weren't yelling at me from across the street.

This is just what I wanted. This was it, all right. Just give my speech. Couldn't be easier. Here I go.

I'm going to just give my speech.

This will be great. No problem. Just walk over and say it. OK, I'm going to do it. I'm going to walk over there. Right over to her. And just say my speech. Just. . .

The bell rang.

I got in line and went into my classroom. Now I had two things to feel bad about. No jacket; no guts. Pitiful.

I'm just pitiful.

I knew I wasn't going to ask her later in the day. It had to be first thing in the morning, or I wouldn't do it at all. And since it hadn't been, I figured it wasn't going to be.

How come Misty couldn't be like some of the other girls I knew? A girl I was working with on a science project said to me, "You going to the dance, Charlie?" and I said, "Yeah."

Then I said to another girl in our group, "You going?" and she said, "Uh-huh." No big deal. No sweat. It happened, and I didn't even realize it had happened until later.

This boy-girl business is *very* confusing. I'm sure nobody has ever had as hard a time as I've had. As I'm having. I don't have it figured out yet. But I'm working on it.

On Tuesday afternoons I have baseball practice. I love baseball. The way a leather mitt smells, the sound of the bat cracking off a base hit—unless I'm pitching—and the way cool grass feels after I've run some laps and fallen facedown in it.

I love standing out on the mound and knowing all the other guys—the whole game—are waiting until I'm ready to throw the next pitch.

When you play baseball you have to do your best, not just for yourself but for everybody else on the team. And to know they're doing their best for you.

Now we were in the league championship game, and we looked good out there. We were ready to do our best.

"What are you, blind?" our first baseman, Paul Nettleton, turning around in the batter's box, asked Mr. McCarthy, our coach. He was umping.

"Pardon me, Nettleton?" he said.

It was too late. Paul knew it.

"Nothing."

"That was a strike, Nettleton," Mr. McCarthy said. "There's nothing wrong with my eyesight that these glasses don't take care of. Two."

He didn't mean two strikes. It was only Paul's first strike. He meant two laps around the field. Not just the diamond we were playing on. The whole field.

Paul dropped his bat and started running.

He knew, as we all did, that there was no point arguing. If you argue, you get four laps. If you keep it up, the whole team gets six.

"So long, Pauly," our second baseman yelled at him. "Try not to run like a spastic."

"Jamal," Mr. McCarthy yelled out to second base. "Two."

"Hey, I didn't—"

"Four!"

Jamal was on his way. He had made a dumb mistake.

Anytime anybody called someone a spaz or geek or dummy, Mr. McCarthy had him out running laps.

We had been playing together for two seasons now, and some guys still fell into that trap. Just one word, the wrong word, and any of us would be on the trail with Paul and Jamal.

Toward the end of practice the Bombers came around and sat up on the bleachers. After we were done I went over to talk to them.

"You Bomber material?" Allen asked me.

"Yeah," I said.

"Maybe. Maybe not."

"I am," I said.

"Not until you pass the initiation, you're not,"

he answered, looking straight at me.

"I am," I said again, hoping I sounded tough. Don't mess with me, man, tough!

"So let's go," he said.

Now? I had to be home for dinner. What if this took a long time? I couldn't say "Yeah, I'm tough, man, but first I have to tell my mommy I'm going to be late for supper."

"Now?" one of the Bombers said to Allen. "It's almost time for me to be home. I get in trouble if I'm late for meals."

The other guys looked at him as if he was really a jerk.

So did I.

"First we're going to the store," Allen said, "and do us a little shopping."

"Right," I said.

We walked over toward a little neighborhood store. Maybe I had to buy everybody Cokes or something. I didn't have any money. This could turn into a real mess.

When we were about half a block away, Allen said, "OK, rookie, I want you to go into the store and steal us a dozen eggs."

What!

"Brian here will be your lookout. He'll distract the guy at the counter while you snag the goods," he said, fists jammed in his pockets.

What size eggs, Allen? You want grade A medium or large or extra large?

I couldn't think of how to stall for time.

"No problem," I said, thinking there were lots of problems with this plan.

"He's chicken," Joey said, seeing the look on my face. "He's so chicken, he can lay his own eggs." He started cackling like a hen.

Everybody laughed. Everybody but me.

"That's a real good imitation," I said. "I guess you must practice that a lot."

It was supposed to be an insult, but it came across like some kind of wienie compliment. At least it shut him up.

"We'll wait here," Allen said, stopping about a quarter of a block from the store. "We'll see if you're Bomber material. Get us some eggs."

Bombs away.

Brian went into the store and started talking to the guy behind the counter. He was new. Maybe about twenty years old. I waited half a minute, and then I went in and headed for the dairy case.

How about yogurt, too, Allen? Man, this was a dumb idea.

I picked up a carton of eggs and was trying to figure out how to get it under my shirt when a voice said, "You doing OK there?"

I dropped the carton.

"Hey, I'm sorry, kid," the guy said—the guy who was supposed to be up at the counter but was now standing right behind me.

Brian had done one crummy job of distracting. I had no idea where he was.

"I . . . I . . . I . . ."

"I'll clean it up, kid," he said in a friendly way.

Great. Thanks, mister, then I'll just rob you and be on my way. The guys are waiting. "Sorry," I said.

"Do I know you?" he asked.

I shrugged my shoulders.

"You're Annie's brother!" he said.

Shoot! Annie again.

"Yeah," I said.

"She's a nice girl."

"Yeah."

"Eggs, huh?" he asked.

"Uh . . ."

"Your mom cooking eggs for dinner?"

"Uh . . . I don't know. She just told me to run down and get some," I lied. Isn't lying better than stealing? I don't mean better. I mean not as bad.

"Yeah," the guy said, "there's nobody madder in the world than a mom who goes to fix supper and finds out she hasn't got something she needs."

"Yeah." What the heck. "She was so mad she forgot to give me money."

"No money! How you going to pay for them?"

I shrugged again.

"Maybe I could leave my baseball glove here until I went home and got some and brought it back," I said.

"What position you play?" he asked.

"Pitcher."

"All right. Good for you. I should have remembered that. Annie told me about some of your games."

She did?

"Here," I said, handing him my glove.

"You keep it," he said. "I trust Annie's brother. You bring in the money later, OK?"

"Yeah," I said. "Thanks."

He handed me a carton of eggs. Extra large.

I stuffed the carton under my shirt just before I walked out of the store. Brian was standing nearby.

"All right, Charlie!" he said.

"Yeah, Brian," I answered. "I really want to thank you for your help."

He nodded as if I really meant it.

"We did it," he said when we got back to where the guys were.

"Nice, Charlie," Allen said.

"So now I'm a Bomber?" I asked.

"Not quite yet. First you have to help us get rid of the eggs."

What, we were going to eat them raw? Gross.

"Your arm sore from practice?" he asked.

"No."

"Good. You're going to need a strong arm."

"I've got a strong arm."

"Good. A strong arm can get an egg all the way from the alley behind the vacant lot over to the front of Old Man Meyer's house."

"Huh?"

"We're going to egg Meyer's house," Joey said to me. "You're chicken *and* stupid."

CHAPTER
5

THE INITIATION

I knew I was in big trouble.

Throwing the eggs would be wrong. If I didn't throw the eggs, I wouldn't get in the Bombers. If I didn't get in the Bombers, I wouldn't get the flight jacket. If I didn't get the jacket, Misty—who had seemed pretty interested in Allen's jacket—wouldn't dance with me at Saturday's dance.

I decided to do the right thing: cop out. As we were walking along, I dropped the carton of eggs. Then Brian stepped on them. "Oh, man!" he whined. "Now look what you did."

"Nice!" I said. "You stepped on the eggs."

"You dropped them, you jerk face."

"You stepped on them, klutz."

"Both of you shut up," Allen told us. He bent down and opened the carton. Six were broken.

Good.

Six weren't.

Bad.

Just my luck to get a carton of the world's toughest eggs.

Allen grabbed my baseball cap and put the six eggs in it. Then he carried it the rest of the way.

We stopped in the alley behind a vacant lot that was overgrown with bushes and tall grass and weeds. You could just barely see Mr. Meyer's house across the street from it.

"We have to do this fast," Allen said. "So nobody has time to call the cops."

Call the cops!

He handed me an egg, and I gave it a little toss. It landed at the front of the lot.

"Quit fooling around," he said. He handed me another one.

I threw it as high as I could. It came down about five feet from where the first one landed.

I dropped the third. It broke.

"Let's go," Joey said. "This guy is a wimp." He

started to leave with some of the others.

Allen glared at me.

I threw three strikes on Mr. Meyer's front door.

Then we ran as fast as we could.

I was in.

I felt awful.

"My man!" Allen said after we got to the garage at his house and shut the door behind us. He put his arm around my shoulder. "Three!"

"Right over the old plate," Brian said.

"Luck," Joey muttered.

"Luck nothing!" Allen said. "This man is a BOMBER!"

He took off his jacket and put it on me.

"Welcome to the club," he said.

"This is for me?"

"Yeah."

"I get to keep your jacket?"

"No. But you can use it. My brother gave me his. It's leather. It's in the house. But I thought it'd be cool if I took my jacket off and like handed it straight to you."

It was cool. I slipped my hands into the pockets. "These are yours," I said, handing him a beat-up pack of cigarettes.

"You want one, man?" he asked.

"No."

"You sure?"

"No. I mean yeah. I mean I'm sure."

I thought maybe he was going to take the jacket back, but he didn't say anything.

"I gotta go!" Brian said. "It's almost seven o'clock."

What! I was an hour late.

"Another wimp," Joey said. "Hey, I gotta split."

Yeah. Some tough guy. I bet he heard his mommy calling, too.

We usually ate at six-thirty, but Mom hadn't served dinner yet when I got home at seven.

"I was a little worried," Dad said when I walked in, "but your mom said the coach probably kept you late to get everybody all set for the championship game."

"I—"

"Wash up."

"OK."

"Where'd you get the jacket?"

"Allen's letting me wear it."

"Uh-huh. Wash up."

What did he mean, "Uh-huh"?

Had Mr. Meyer called them? Had he seen me? Had someone else? Had they called the cops? Had the cops called Mom and Dad? What did he mean, "Uh-huh"?

Then Dad shouted to me, "I thought maybe you'd be eating eggs this evening."

"I can explain. . . ," I mumbled.

"Your mother said if we had to start without you, there probably wouldn't be anything left when you got here, and she'd have to fix you a couple of scrambled eggs. Good thing we waited, huh?"

"Yeah, Dad," I yelled back.

"Bet you're hungry."

No, Dad, I thought. Not really.

Mom wouldn't let me wear my new jacket during dinner. Afterward I walked back up to the store to pay for the eggs.

Rhonda let me borrow the money. Mostly in nickels and pennies from her Winnie-the-Pooh bank.

I went back to the store and handed the guy his money.

"A few eggs can go a long ways, huh?" he asked me.

"What?"

"I mean feeding a family."

"Yeah."

I stopped on my way out and looked at a couple of hot-rod magazines.

"They aren't worth it," he said.

I wondered if he was talking about the magazines.

I woke up early Wednesday morning, put my Bomber jacket on, and went back to bed.

I woke up later to see Annie standing beside my bed and laughing at me.

I told her to get lost.

She stuck out her tongue at me and left.

I got to school early but didn't see Misty. I found out later she was sick that day. Things were not going great, considering I was now a member of this hotshot club.

After school, Annie had bowling practice, just like every Wednesday afternoon, and Mom had to take Soap and Water to get new shoes.

I don't know why Mom couldn't do that after dinner, but I said I'd go with Annie because I was trying to be especially good, knowing that at any minute the cops might pull up and slap handcuffs on me for the Great Egg (Mis)Adventure.

I didn't really think they'd handcuff me. Would they? Probably not.

But Mom and Dad would make me stay in my room until I was twenty-one.

Annie and I had to walk to the bowling alley, and I had to stay there until she was done. Not a great afternoon.

This was another of those cases where I'm the oldest but I'm not really the oldest. Here I was, watching out for Annie, and she's two years older than I am. But I've been doing this since I was five, if not longer. That's just the first time I remember doing it.

Annie loves to bowl. She's one of the best on her team. Her career high score is a 27. She is not a great bowler.

Her team really stinks. But they have a lot of fun. They are a Special Olympics team. That's an organization that sets up games for people like Annie. They have tournaments and state and national and even international games and give out medals and stuff.

Annie has bowled and thrown the softball and run a little track.

Anyway, her team was practicing that Wednesday afternoon for a regional contest on Saturday at one o'clock, the same day as my baseball championship game, which was at ten. That made me a little mad. Her stuff always crowds in on mine.

We live about four blocks from the bowling alley, and we got there without anybody I know seeing us. Inside, there were ten or twelve other people on her team changing into bowling shoes and trying to find the perfect ball and just generally messing around.

I was supposed to wait until Annie was done and then walk back home with her. Like her baby-sitter.

"I'm going to get a strike for you, Chuckie," she said when we got there.

"Great," I answered.

"Mary Louise Matthews isn't going to get a strike today."

"Uh-huh."

"I'm going to beat her."

"Yeah. Get your shoes and find a ball."

She had learned to tie her own shoes in the past year, and it still took her a long time. I knew she had to hustle if she was going to be ready when it was time for practice to start.

"Hi, Jill!" she yelled out to her coach, who was on the other side of the lobby.

Jill waved.

Kids who were hanging out by the video games stared at Annie and at me. I tried to pretend I didn't notice.

Mary Louise Matthews noticed us.

"Hi, pig," she said to Annie.

"Shut up," Annie said.

Mary Louise was a year or two older than Annie

and a lot bigger. The two of them had been placing first and second in practice all season. Right now Annie was top bowler, and that really ticked off Mary Louise. She had won a gold medal in last year's contest. She wore it around her neck at every practice. She didn't like Annie at all.

"I'm not a pig," Annie said to me. "She is."

"Get your shoes tied," I said.

"She's a big fat pig."

"With a curly tail. Come on, Annie. Hurry up." I bet those were my first words instead of "Mama" or "Dada": "Come on, Annie. Hurry up."

"I'm gonna beat you," Mary Louise said while she continued to hunt for the ball she was going to use.

"Uh-uh," Annie said.

"Uh-huh."

"Uh-uh."

"Uh-huh."

"Uh-uh."

"Uh-huh."

"UH-UH!"

"UH-HUH!"

"Shut up, Annie," I said.

"Let's go, girls!" their coach yelled over our way.

"See? You're late," I said to Annie.

"I'm gonna beat Mary Louise."

"Great," I said.

They were using two lanes way down by the far wall. Far away from the video games and the kids hanging out by them, I was glad to see.

There was no telling when someone I knew might walk in, and there I would be.

Jill and somebody's mom had the group divided on two lanes. They had Annie and Mary Louise separated.

Very smart move.

Most of the bowlers were older than Annie. Some were grown up. Some didn't have Down's syndrome, but they were retarded anyway.

They just looked . . . odd. Maybe not if you just saw them and they were dressed OK. Which they weren't. They had on some weird clothes. Like one guy always wore a vest covered with buttons that had sayings and stuff on them. And another always wore a wool stocking cap. Even inside. And they acted more like kids than grown-ups. They talked that way, too.

Some of them still lived at home with their families. Some lived in a group home. That's a house where all kinds of handicapped people live together with some other people who take care of them.

The team was a goofy-looking bunch. But, as I said, they had a lot of fun, even though they didn't bowl worth beans.

They were all more concerned with the rack behind their seats. It was a long shelf that had a lot of holes in it, each hole big enough for a soda pop can. Just about everyone had a can of something. Orange seemed to be the favorite.

Annie came away with the day's highest score, a big 25 in the second game. She didn't get a strike, but she almost got a spare. On the way home she wet her pants.

I thought I saw Misty walking toward us, about a block away, and I made Annie go with me and take the long way home, a long way I had just invented.

After I thought about it, I decided it probably wasn't Misty. She was home sick that day. But you never know.

It was a close call.

CHAPTER
6

A CRUMMY PRACTICE AND A WORSE OPEN HOUSE

M isty was back at school on Thursday. I saw her first thing that morning.

I zipped up my jacket halfway and . . . I zipped up Allen's jacket halfway and figured I looked pretty sharp.

She was talking with some other girls.

I watched her until the bell rang.

After school, the team had practice. We were all a little nervous about Saturday's game.

"Men," Mr. McCarthy said at the beginning of practice, "I want you to remember one thing. You will either win or lose on Saturday. Either way, the sun will still come up on Sunday."

"I think that's two things," Jamal said, and everybody laughed.

I quit laughing when I saw her heading toward the field.

Not her, Misty. Her, Annie.

"HI, CHUCKIE! HI, CHUCKIE'S TEAM!"

The guys all saw her. Some of them waved. Some didn't do anything.

"I need to talk to her," I said to the coach, and he nodded.

I ran over to her so she wouldn't get any closer to the team.

"Mom said I could come here," Annie said when I got to her.

"You can't walk all the way here by yourself."

"They're at the swings."

"Who?"

"Mom. And the little girls."

"Why don't you go swing, Annie?"

"I want to watch you."

"Well, you can't."

"I let you watch me."

"I didn't want to."

"Mom said."

"I don't care what Mom said. You can't watch me."

"I'm telling."

"Great. Go tell Mom."

And I meant, Go. Tell Mom.

"Social hour is over, Charlie," the coach yelled at me.

Sometimes I think my life is filled with yelling. "OK!" I shouted back.

"I'm going to watch," Annie said to me.

"No."

"Why?"

"I don't want you around me."

She looked confused. More confused than usual. Then she looked like she was going to cry.

"Let's go, Charlie!" the coach hollered.

"I got to get back to practice," I said, and she didn't say anything. "Maybe next week you and I can play catch and—"

"Shut up."

"I'm trying to be nice, Annie."

"Shut up."

"I just don't want you watching me while . . ."

"Shut up."

"Ah, you shut up."

"You shut up."

"You."

"You."

She makes me so mad sometimes. I feel like I'm

four years old again. I turned and walked away.

My pitching was really crummy.

When I finally looked back that way, she was gone. Good. I never asked her to come watch me practice. I didn't want her to. Don't I get to decide anything?

The batters kept getting hits off me. Finally Mr. McCarthy took me off the mound and put our third baseman up there. He's the backup pitcher. He fanned three batters.

"What's the problem, Charlie?" the coach asked me over by the first-base fence.

"Nothing."

"How come everybody got a hit off you?"

"I don't know."

"You want to play Saturday?"

"Yeah."

"You want to start Saturday's game?"

He wasn't going to let me start? I had started practically all the games this season.

"Yeah," I said, really paying attention for the first time.

"What's the problem?" he asked again.

"I can't concentrate."

"You have to concentrate."

"I keep thinking about . . . other things."

"A pitcher has to concentrate."

"I know."

"There's only him and the batter."

"Yeah."

"And maybe a runner on first."

"Uh-huh."

"And second and third if things aren't going too well."

I guess that was a joke.

Then he said, "I saw an interview on TV with Ricardo 'The Hammer' Fernandez a couple weeks ago. You know who he is?"

Of course I knew. "Relief pitcher for the Dodgers."

"He had just pitched the final two and a third innings and won the game. Nobody got a hit, and he had five strikeouts."

"Uh-huh."

"The guy who was doing the interview said Ricardo looked a little concerned out there. He asked him what was going through his mind. You know what Ricardo said?"

I shook my head.

"He said that while he was on the mound, he thought about getting through the inning. Not one batter at a time—one pitch at a time. He was having a lot of fun. But as soon as he stepped off the mound, he was really worried that he had left the lights on in his car and that his battery would be dead when he finally got back out to the parking lot."

The coach patted me on the side of the arm and started to leave.

I didn't get it. He looked at my face and saw I didn't get it.

"Everybody's got troubles, Charlie," he said. "When you're pitching, go out there and have fun. Your troubles will be waiting for you when you step off the mound. You don't need to drag them around with you."

"It's . . ." I was going to say "Annie."

He waited.

"OK," I said finally and walked away.

He had no idea what I was going through.

That night, we had Mom's homemade burgers and fries for dinner, but we had to eat fast because we were going to the open house at the middle school.

I thought I looked pretty good. My favorite jeans, a cool shirt, and my Bomber jacket.

When I came down from my room to the living room, I saw the twins wearing good clothes, and I became very nervous.

Then Dad yelled at Annie to hurry up, and I got scared.

"Where are they going?" I asked him.

"What do you mean, 'Where are they going?'"

Uh-oh. "I thought Mrs. Petrovich was coming over," I said. She was our baby-sitter.

"Why?"

"To watch Annie and Pots and Pans."

"The open house is tonight, Charlie," Dad said.

"And you and Mom and I are going."

"It's for the whole family."

"No, it isn't."

"That's what the invitation said."

"No, it didn't."

"Sure it did. We all want to see where you'll be going next year. This is pretty exciting stuff."

And getting more exciting all the time. "I don't want Annie to go."

"What?"

"I don't think Annie and the little girls should go."

"Why not?"

Why not? Because people I know will be there, that's why not. "I don't know," I answered.

He looked at me funny. And kind of sadly. "We'd all like to come," he said. And he emphasized "all."

"Sometimes—"

"I can't find my shoe!" Annie screamed.

"Do you have one?" Dad called up to her.

"Yeah!"

"Look around where that one was."

"It's on my foot!"

"Look where you found it."

"I didn't find it. It's on my foot."

"Dr. Jekyll and Mr. Hyde," Dad said to the twins, who were out in the dining room.

"What?" they answered together.

"Go help Annie find her shoe."

They scurried off.

He turned back to me, and his face said, Yes? You were saying?

"I'll wait outside," I said.

He nodded.

I was good and nervous by the time we got to the middle school. It's a lot different from the elementary school. I had been in the building before, but never when I was going to be going there. It made a big difference.

There were, I don't know, maybe four hundred or five hundred people sitting in the gymnasium when we got there—all of us.

I walked in fast and was lucky to spot an empty chair by some guys from my class. I ran over and sat with them.

Mom and Dad and Annie and the twins found a

place to sit up on the bleachers.

A couple of the guys told me again how much they liked my jacket. I kept my hands in my pockets and shrugged my shoulders. I was looking good.

The seventh-grade band played "Yankee Doodle" and "Louie, Louie." They sounded OK.

Then the principal got up and said how much he appreciated everybody coming tonight and what a great place this school was and how much spirit there was and he knew everybody was going to have a great time next year.

Kind of boring.

Then he introduced the vice-principal, who was in charge of discipline, and that guy said if anybody messed around at *this* school he'd know about it and he would take appropriate action.

The principal had been all smiles; this guy didn't even have one.

Then the band played some kind of marching song, and the principal got back up and said we were free to wander around the classrooms and meet teachers and stuff.

I was looking forward to that until he added that we had to stay with our families. He didn't want bunches of students wandering around alone. He smiled when he said it, but the vice-principal was standing right behind him. The VP hadn't smiled yet.

Then everybody got up to leave, and the guys I was with found their folks. Some had come with their brothers and sisters. Some hadn't. I just stood there until I couldn't ignore Mom waving her arm anymore.

"Where do you want to go first?" she asked me.

"I don't know."

"Come on. This is your big night."

It seemed to me that lots of people were staring at Annie. Even lots of kids my age that I didn't know. Four different grade schools sent students here. I just wanted to melt into the crowd for a while.

Two years or so.

"How about the wood shop?" Dad asked. "You're good at that."

I knew that's where some of the Bombers would be.

"I don't think . . ."

"Come on," Mom said. "I know just where it is." And she pointed at the little map she had picked up when she came into the gym.

"I loved wood shop," Dad said. Dad works in an office, but I think maybe he'd rather be building junk. He knows the names of all the tools at the hardware store and what they're for. A couple years ago, when I was in the Cub Scouts, he and I had made a birdhouse together.

I had to quit the Scouts. Annie had a lot of doctors' appointments around then, and I had to sit in the waiting room with the twins while she and Mom went in. The twins weren't even two years old then. It wasn't much fun.

The birdhouse is still in a tree out in our backyard. I don't think any birds ever made a nest in it. Anyway, that night Dad looked so happy thinking about me learning more about making stuff out of wood.

"OK?" he asked.

I didn't say anything.

"OK!" he said. "Lead the way, ladies."

You know how when you're working on a computer and you do something wrong, the screen flashes "ERROR! ERROR! ERROR!"?

That was what my brain was doing.

Allen and all the other guys would be in the wood shop. And Annie was heading that way. With me.

ERROR!

We were walking down a hallway, getting closer and closer. My mind was spinning so fast, coming up with nothing, that I didn't even see

Misty and her folks walking toward us until it was too late.

She wasn't more than five feet away. She was looking at her map.

I was doomed.

"I smell cookies!" Annie yelled, and I turned my face toward a wall of lockers and kept walking.

"In here," I heard a man say to Misty. "This is the science lab."

I guess they turned into that room. I wasn't watching.

"I want a cookie!" Annie said.

The smell was coming from the room where they teach cooking and sewing and stuff like that.

I knew I had to get away, so I said I had to go to the bathroom and spent about ten minutes in there. When I came out I found Mom and Dad and the girls and said I wanted to get some fresh air. They finished their tour. I snuck outside and sat on the ground between our car and some other car, where I was pretty sure no one could see me.

Later Mom said I didn't look well.

Dad said that even though middle school can be pretty scary, he was sure I would do fine.

Annie said she wanted another cookie.

CHAPTER
7

I Do Something
Very Dumb

By later that night I'd convinced myself that Misty hadn't seen Annie. That she hadn't associated Annie with me. I was sure of it. Pretty sure.

But I wasn't ready for Friday morning. I was standing out on the playground before school wearing my flight jacket, even though it was already pretty warm. Well, it wasn't that warm. There was kind of a cool breeze.

As I was standing there thinking about how my life was crumbling around me, somebody said "Hi."

I turned around and there she was.

Misty.

I said, "Abba abba abba." Not quite as cool as the breeze.

But she just smiled. "How are you?" she asked.

"Fine," I squeaked.

How had she snuck up on me again? I remembered the fable about the mice trying to put a bell on the cat. Misty needed a bell.

I couldn't take this. I wasn't ready. There she was. She was sure pretty. She smelled good, too. "How come you have a jacket on?" she asked.

She'd noticed!

"Did your mom sew these on?" she asked.

"What?"

"The patches on your sleeves." She examined the little flag closely. "This kind of sewing is really hard to do," she said. "I can never get it right."

"I'm in a club," I said. I was going to add, "The Bombers," but she said "Oh" before I had a chance to, and her "Oh" kind of ended the conversation. That part of it, anyway.

Hey, babe, how about a slow dance? popped into my head. The possibility of my saying that was as likely as my suddenly flapping my arms and taking off in flight. No way.

"I have a question for you," she said.

Annie! I just knew it. Rats! I was thinking fast of ways to deny I even knew my older sister.

I could say

—"Who?"

—"Last night?"

—"Open house?"

—"I'm an only child."

—"Do you always smell this good?"

It was getting hotter. I was getting hotter. Not "cool" hot. Sweat hot.

"Are you . . ." she began.

I just knew she was going to finish with "related to that girl I saw you with at the middle school last night?" Just knew it. I didn't even need to listen to her question. "I'm not sure who you mean," I answered, and she just stared at me.

"You," she said.

"Me?"

She started to look embarrassed and said, "Never mind."

Then I said, "What was your question again?"

"The dance. Will I see you there?"

"Abba abba abba." That's the way it came out, but what I meant was, "You bet! I'll see you there, Misty!"

She said, "What?"

I tried again, and it came out "Yeah," and she

said "Good" and "Me, too" and gave me a little smile and sort of ran away.

Yes. YES! YESSSSSSS!

She had given me a little smile. Just for me. Not little "small." Little "cute." Little "pretty." Little "beautiful."

She and I.

She was going to the dance. I was going to the dance. We were going to the dance.

Maybe, just maybe, we were going to dance together. It was possible. Anything was possible.

I hadn't been wasting all those afternoons in my room boogying in front of the mirror with the radio on. I had been preparing. I was ready.

She'd given me a smile. She—

"ROOKIE!"

She—

"HEY, ROOKIE!"

She—

Something hit me in the side of the head. It was a book. Joey had thrown it. I was surprised. Where did he get a book?

The guys were standing over by the fence.

"Rookie," Allen said, "who you talking to?"

"Huh?"

"I said, 'Who are you talking to?'"

"Nobody."

"Right. The jacket looks good on you."

"Thanks."

"You want to keep it?"

Huh? "Yeah," I said.

"Good. Part two of the initiation is tonight."

"You already initiated me." Just ask Mr. Meyer.

"That was only the first part, retard," Joey said. "Gimme my book back."

I picked it up and threw it at him. He missed the catch.

"Good hands," I said.

"Shut up."

"Tonight," Allen said. "After supper. You can go out, right?"

It was light out until almost eight o'clock this time of the year. "Yeah."

"Meet us at the vacant lot."

"Throwing eggs is stupid," I said.

"Throwing eggs is kids' stuff," he answered.

I don't know why I can't just have something good happen to me and let it stop there. Misty was going to the dance.

She had asked *me* if I was going.

That had felt so good it made the thought of another initiation seem even worse.

If throwing eggs was for kids, what was for tough guys like the Bombers? My Language Arts teachers have told me I have a very good imagination, but I couldn't imagine what Allen had in mind.

That's not true. I could. I didn't want to. I wouldn't let myself.

I just wanted to stand around and talk to Misty and not say "Abba abba abba" but something intelligent and get another smile. Get a whole bunch of smiles. I don't ask for a lot. It's not fair.

So all that day, instead of thinking about the dance and her or even the championship baseball game I had to pitch the next morning, I kept thinking about the initiation. You ever try to *not* think about something like that? Good luck.

That night at dinner Dad said, "You worried about the game?"

I almost said, "What game?"

After we ate I said, "I'm going to go outside for a little bit."

"Just ten minutes. We have to go to Annie's school," Mom said.

"Huh?" That was the first I'd heard of that. I think I would have remembered having to go to Annie's school.

"Tonight is her open house."

Oh, no! "Is Mrs. Petro—"

"We're all going."

No! I couldn't believe it.

"Annie wants us to."

No, no, no . . . yes! That meant I couldn't go out with the Bombers. "OK," I said. "I'll be back in ten minutes."

I ran to the vacant lot. Allen and a couple of the guys were there. Some hadn't shown up yet.

"I can't go tonight," I said.

"Chicken," Joey said, and he spat on the ground.

"I have to go out with my family," I told Allen.

"Have to?" he asked.

"Yeah."

"Don't you want to keep that jacket?"

"Yeah."

"Become a real Bomber?"

"Yeah."

"Well, Charlie, I don't know. You don't act like you want to."

"I do."

"We were all going to add to the club's car-accessory collection."

"Huh?"

"Swipe hubcaps and break off antennas," Joey said. "Stupid."

He meant me. Not the idea.

I thought the idea was. And me. If I went along

with it. But I didn't have to. "Shoot," I said. "I can't. I gotta go to another open house."

"That was last night," Joey said. "Where were you?"

"I was there," I said. "Where were you? Baking cookies?"

He took a step toward me, and Allen put his arm out between us. "Knock it off."

That was probably what Joey had in mind.

"What open house?" Allen asked.

"At another school."

He looked interested.

"What school?"

"A different school."

"*What* school?"

"Annie's school."

"That's different, all right," Joey said, and he laughed. So did some of the other guys.

"Maybe you don't have to miss the initiation," Allen said.

Allen could think fast. They weren't nice thoughts, but they came fast. He told us his new plan. It sounded worse than breaking off car antennas to me. I said I'd do it.

"Hi, Ms. Donaldson!" Annie screamed as soon as we got into her classroom.

"Hi, Annie."

"My family came to see my room."

"I see that."

"This is my desk," she said to us.

"Nice, Annie," Dad said.

"And this is Peter's, and this is Angela's, and she doesn't have a chair."

"Why?" Rhoda asked.

"Because she has one," Annie said.

Great. What was that supposed to mean?

"What kind does Angela have, Annie?" Ms. Donaldson asked.

"With wheels."

"A wheelchair."

"Wheelchair."

"So she doesn't need a chair at her desk, does she, Annie?"

"Uh-uh. I made that picture." She was pointing at the bulletin board. The drawings looked like a kindergarten class had done them.

"Good," Mom said. "Very pretty. Isn't it, Charlie?"

"Yeah, sure," I said. But what I was thinking was, the back door. By the girls' rest room. I kept saying it to myself.

There were lots of families at the open house. The school has one in the fall and one in the spring.

The kids at Annie's school have all different kinds of handicaps. Some of them used to gross me out when I was younger. There were kids who drooled and kids who talked funny and a kid with flippers instead of arms and lots of weird-looking kids.

When we were done seeing Annie's classroom, I said I had to go to the bathroom, and I went to the back door Allen had checked out the day before. I pushed the metal bar and opened the door a crack.

"Thanks, Bomber," Allen whispered to me from the alley.

"I can't believe he did it," Joey said.

"Shut up!" Allen hissed, and he stuck an end of a rolled-up newspaper in the door so it didn't shut all the way.

Then I didn't hear anything. Except the rattle a can of spray paint makes when somebody is shaking it.

CHAPTER
8

THE CHAMPIONSHIP GAME, THE TOURNAMENT, AND THE DANCE

I couldn't fall asleep that night. I kept thinking about the Bombers. Wondering what they had done. What we had done. What I had done.

It kept getting later and later: 11:21, 11:46, 12:03, 1:35. Maybe I slept between the times I looked at my clock. Finally I did sleep for sure, but I had dreams about graffiti and Annie and the ball game and Misty.

I woke up at 5:36 and was glad morning had come and it was light out.

At breakfast I told Dad I didn't want Annie at my game. I said I couldn't concentrate when she was there. He said he understood and he'd take care of it. He would be the only one there. Mom would stay with Annie and the twins. They wished me good luck. Annie insisted on giving me a kiss.

When Dad and I got to the field, most of the team was already there, and they looked as nervous as I felt.

"No sweat," our catcher, Bob Carbonetti, said.

"Yeah," Jamal added.

"We'll whup 'em," Paul said.

But they didn't look too sure.

Bob was helping me get loose while Mr. McCarthy watched.

"You look a little ragged," the coach said to me.

I felt a lot ragged.

"Your pitching is OK. It's you that looks a little off. Maybe it's just nerves."

"Yes, sir."

"Take a break, Carbonetti," he said.

After Bob had gone, Mr. McCarthy looked over at the bleachers and said, "Where's your family?"

"My dad's here."

"The rest couldn't make it?"

I shrugged.

"Now are you going to concentrate?" he asked.

I shrugged again.

"Would it be that bad having Annie here?"

"Worse than you can imagine," I blurted out.

"I can imagine. Come on. We'll walk the field."

We started out along the edge of the outfield.

"It's not easy having a sister with a disabling condition, is it?"

"No, sir."

"It's not easy having a brother with one, either."

I didn't say anything.

"Did I ever tell you about my brother Patrick?"

"Uh-uh."

"He's a city council member in another state. A small city. More like a big town, really. But it's the county seat."

"Uh-huh," I said.

"He's blind," Mr. McCarthy said. "He had trouble breathing when he was first born, and the doctors put him in an oxygen tent and gave him too much oxygen and blinded him. People back then didn't know that could happen."

He had my attention.

"I was six years old when he was born. I remember how much it changed my family. It seemed to me that after that my parents had time only for Pat. He needed extra care, he needed extra medical attention, he needed extra love. I felt like he took all the care, all the attention, and all the love my folks had to give."

We kept walking. I was glad he didn't expect me to say anything.

"A lot of people said my mom and dad should have put Pat in an institution. Do you know what that is?"

"A special school where kids stay all the time."

"Kids and adults. My parents said no. Instead, we all had to take turns reading to him. We were his eyes. And he had special tutors. And special books in college."

"He went to college?" I asked.

"And on to law school. He became a lawyer. But some people with a disabling condition can never live independently. They go to a group home and work in a sheltered workshop, a place that's got jobs they can handle. That may be where Annie is heading."

I just kept listening.

"I feel differently about it now that I'm grown up," he said, "but when I was a kid, sometimes I wished my parents would put him in an institution. Then I'd hate myself for feeling that way. I'd feel guilty about it. Some choice, huh? Feel mad or bad or guilty. I loved my brother, and sometimes I hated him. You aren't the first one to go through this, you know."

I didn't know.

"Why do you think I won't let you or the other boys say anything that makes fun of people in a mean way?"

"Because of your brother," I said.

"Yeah," he said. "Most people just don't know any better. But I do. My brother taught me that. He made me a better person, and I like the guy. He's my brother."

We won the game. Dad said it was the best I ever pitched. When I was on the mound, I didn't think about what Mr. McCarthy had said. I just thought about each pitch. Each out. Each inning.

It felt nice to win, but it didn't seem as important as I thought it might. Still, it was really neat to get a trophy for being Most Valuable Player. Me! MVP!

Dad even bought me a hamburger and stuff on the way home. He said he was very proud of me. Said I deserved the trophy.

By then I couldn't stop thinking about what Mr. McCarthy had said. It would be nice to be big enough and have enough power so that if you heard someone call a person "retardo," you could make them go run laps.

It would be very nice.

There wasn't time for me to take a shower or change when we got home. We pulled up in the driveway, and Mom and Annie and Waffles and

Syrup came out of the house and got in the car.

Annie was pretty excited about her tournament. She really wanted a gold medal. Especially after seeing my trophy.

"I'm going to win a medal," she said to Mary Louise Matthews, her number one enemy, as soon as we got in the lobby of the bowling alley.

"He dresses funny," Mary Louise answered, pointing at me in my baseball uniform.

"Shut up," Annie said.

All the bowlers on Annie's team were checking in with their coach, and finding the right ball and getting their shoes and just messing around, having fun.

I could tell Annie was nervous. She hadn't screamed hello to anyone.

"You'll do great," I said to her, but she wasn't paying attention to me.

There were maybe fifteen teams there. Almost two hundred bowlers.

Some man walked halfway down a center lane and turned around and faced the crowd and said, "I want to welcome all of you to this year's regional tournament. I know the athletes are eager to start."

The bowlers cheered, and so did the crowd. So did I.

"Please stand for the singing of the national anthem," the man said.

Everybody stood up. A lot of the bowlers were already standing. Each team was supposed to be in the little area reserved for their lane, and there weren't enough seats there for everybody on a team. While some people came out with the American flag, Mary Louise pushed past a couple other teammates and stood next to Annie.

Big trouble.

Most people were watching a tiny woman in a lime green bowling shirt who was going to lead the singing.

"Oh, say can you see . . ."

Mary Louise turned around and pointed at me and made a goofy face, and I heard Annie say "Shut up."

". . . at the twilight's last gleaming . . ."

Mary Louise didn't shut up. She kept pointing and laughing. I guess she thought my uniform pants and long stockings were a riot.

"SHUT UP!"

I thought everybody would hear that.

". . . and the rockets' red glare . . ."

Annie and Mary Louise started pushing each other—hard. Then Mary Louise pretended to toss her bowling ball at Annie's feet. Annie picked up an open can of Orange Fizz somebody had left sitting in the pop rack for safekeeping.

It wasn't safe.

Neither was Mary Louise.

Annie was really ticked off.

I knew she was going to dump it on Mary Louise. We used to do that a lot to each other when we were little. But Mary Louise just grabbed the can and smashed it down on Annie's forehead.

All of this happened very fast.

Jill finally noticed, and some people separated the two of them, but by now bright red blood was streaming down Annie's face.

". . . and the home of the brave?"

Everybody cheered.

We took Annie to the emergency room at the hospital. She had to have two stitches.

She missed the tournament. She didn't get a medal. And she was still mad at Mary Louise for saying I dressed stupid.

Annie wore the bandage on her forehead as if it were a medal. Something she was proud of.

I can still see the scar.

I think I always will.

It had been a pretty full day, and it wasn't over yet. I still had the dance.

But first I had to take care of some business.

I got dressed real sharp and grabbed my Bomber jacket and said good-bye to everybody. It was decided that I would walk over to the school and Mom or Dad would pick me up at ten when the dance was over.

I stopped by Allen's house. I didn't go in. I didn't even ring the doorbell. I just left the jacket on his front porch.

Joey had been right all along. I wasn't Bomber material.

I was walking toward school when I ran into Brian, the Bomber who had seen the root beer incident.

"Hi," he said.

"Hi," I said, and for the first time in what seemed like a long time I thought of the sound a can of spray paint makes when you shake it. That rattle.

"How did last night go?" I asked.

"Crummy," Brian said. "Joey screwed up and pulled out the paper Allen had jammed in the door, and the door locked."

"So you guys didn't—"

"Then we were going to paint stuff on the outside of the building, but a cop car drove by and saw us, and we ran and Allen ditched the paint—so that was the end of that."

"Too bad," I lied.

"Yeah, I guess," he said and shrugged. "See ya."

"See ya," I said.

I was kind of glad I got a little time to myself. I walked the rest of the way to school but didn't go inside. Instead I just stopped and looked around. I had spent seven years of my life here. Kindergarten through sixth grade. I would be going through a graduation ceremony here in a couple of days. Everything would change. Someone tapped me on the shoulder. It was Misty.

"Abba abba abba." Life was never perfect. She just laughed. Really sweet. Sometimes life was very close to perfect.

"Sorry I make you nervous," she said.

"It's OK," I answered. She looked so good. I think I already mentioned she smelled good. "You want to go in?" I asked, surprising myself that I got all those words out.

"Not right away."

"OK."

"I saw you at the open house," Misty said.

No, No, No! "Oh?" Was she hiding in the boys' bathroom, too? Did she see me down between the cars? In the hallway! I *knew* it!

"I'm a tutor there, once a week," she said. "With a couple of other Girl Scouts."

"At Annie's school? Where my sister goes?" I asked.

"Yeah. The kid I work with is just a peewee. Third grade. He has CP."

"Seepy?" I asked, making it rhyme with "sleepy."

"Not 'seepy.' C P—cerebral palsy."

"What's that?"

"His brain won't tell his body how to do stuff. He's in a wheelchair."

"My sister has Down syndrome. She's mentally retarded."

"I know."

The rest of the evening didn't get any better. And it didn't get any worse. It just stayed that great. There weren't any slow dances. We danced a couple dances together. Mostly we just talked.

A few days later Coach McCarthy stopped by my house and spoke with my parents about his brother. Later in the summer Mom and Dad got me signed up to join a "siblings' group." The group is for kids about my age who have a brother or sister with some kind of disabling condition.

There are a lot of us. Don't mess with us, boy!

We meet once a month. It was after our last

meeting, toward the end of summer, that I decided to give Annie my trophy. I got some masking tape and put her name over the place where it said "Little League Tournament," but I didn't cover up "Most Valuable Player."

"This is for you," I said. "It was kind of my fault you didn't get to be in the bowling tournament."

"It's got a boy with a thing on top of it," she said.

"A bat."

"I don't like baseball."

"See? I put your name here. Most Valuable Player."

"This looks stupid." She had a point.

I laughed. I could tell that really confused her. It confused me, too. I still have a lot of confusing thoughts, but I am sure of one thing.

I love her.

I'll always love my sister Annie.

Bill Dodds has three children, the oldest of whom has learning disabilities. Mr. Dodds is a volunteer in the Special Olympics and other advocacy groups for retarded citizens. He is the author of *The Hidden Fortune,* a middle-grade novel. He lives with his wife and family in Mountlake Terrace, Washington.